BEAR AT THE BEACH

North-South Books

NEW YORK | LONDON

Bear
at the Beach

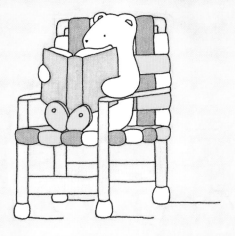

WRITTEN AND ILLUSTRATED BY

Clay Carmichael

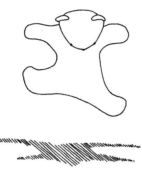

First published in the United States, Great Britain, Canada,
Australia, and New Zealand in 1996 by North-South Books,
an imprint of Nord-Süd Verlag AG, Gossau Zürich, Switzerland.

Published in the United States by North-South Books Inc., New York.

Library of Congress Cataloging-in-Publication Data is available.
ISBN 1-55858-569-9 (TRADE BINDING)
1 3 5 7 9 TB 10 8 6 4 2
ISBN 1-55858-570-2 (LIBRARY BINDING)
1 3 5 7 9 LB 10 8 6 4 2
A CIP catalogue record for this book is available
from The British Library.

*The art for this book was prepared with
pen-and-ink and watercolor.*

Printed in Belgium

to Bear

nce on an island in a house by the sea,
there was a bear who wanted a father.

He lived with Clara, who loved him. They played every day in the turtle-green sea.

He shared her strawberries for
breakfast, her yellow umbrella and

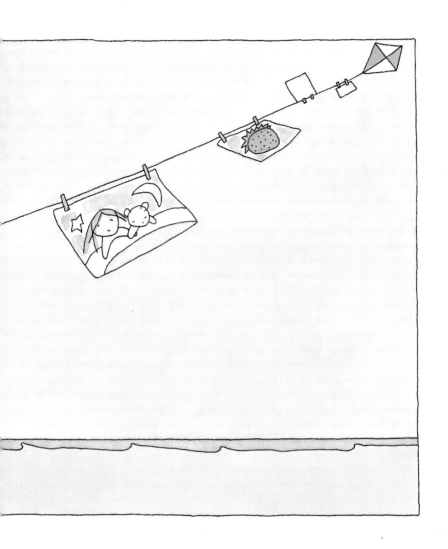

paint box in the afternoon, and her
big bed at night.

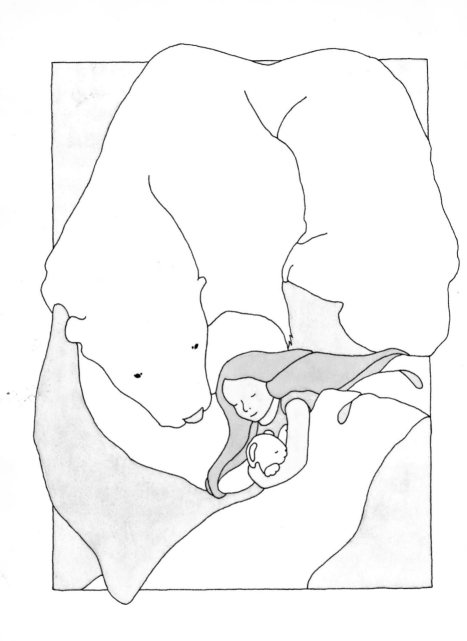

But every night as he slept in her arms, he dreamed of having a father. And soon his dream became a longing. And then his longing became an empty place inside him he thought only a father could fill.

"If only my father would come," Bear sighed, and stared sadly out to sea.

"Maybe you have to ask him," Clara said.

So they sent his father message after
message in paper ships on the outgoing
tide, and searched the sea rim all day
for any sign of his sail, and strung shell
chimes together with tooth floss to
guide him safely ashore at night. But no
father came.

"Maybe I have to find him," Bear
said, and set out along the shore.

"Have you seen my father?" he asked the sea.

"What's your father like?" she said.

"Someone I can tell my secrets to," said Bear.

"No, little bear," she whispered, "I've never met anyone I trusted as much as that."

"Have you seen my father?" he asked the fish.

"What's your father like?" she said.

"He plays with me, and teaches me things, and explains when I don't understand," said Bear.

"No, little bear," she said, "I've never met anyone as wise and as wonderful as that."

"Have you seen my father?" he asked the ducks.

"What's your father like?" they said.

"Someone who loves me just as I am," said Bear.

"Sorry, little bear," they said, "no one's ever loved us as much as that."

"Have you seen my father?" he asked
a clam.

"What's your father like?" the clam
said.

"Someone who holds me in the night
and says, 'There, there, little bear, it
was only a dream.'"

"Why don't you take a nap," said the
clam, "and see if anyone turns up?"

Bear slept till late afternoon. But what turned up only made him crabby.

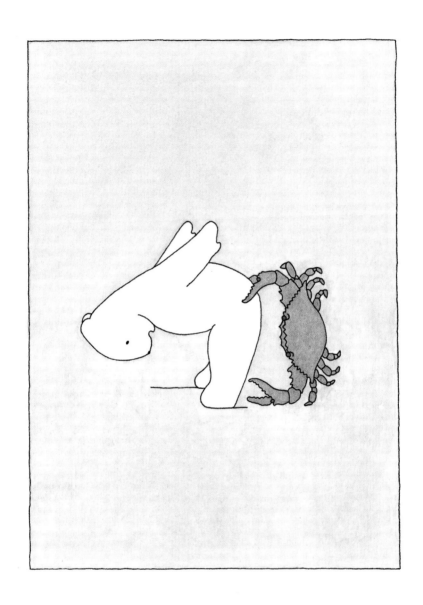

"Have you seen my father?" he asked a boy building a castle.

"Only mine," said the boy. "What's yours like?"

"He's my best friend," Bear said. "And I'm his."

"Well," said the boy, "if you can't find him, maybe you could make one."

So Bear made a father out of sand, just like the one he had always wanted. "I love you, Daddy," he said, and kissed his father's nose.

But the tide came in, as tides do,
and little by little washed his father
into the sea.

It is a hard thing to watch your father
wash away. It made Bear cry.

"There, there, little bear," said a teeny tiny voice inside his father's head. Out popped a hermit crab.

"Don't worry," said the hermit. "Your father will be back, you'll see."

They waited together until the sun went down and the moon rose and stars dotted the sky.

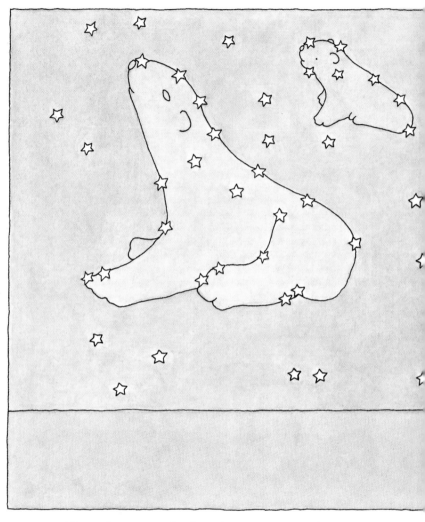

"Look!" said the hermit. "There's
your father! And there you are too!"
"Oh!" said Bear. It was the most

beautiful sight he had ever seen.

"Daddy!" he cried. "Come down and play with me!"

"He can't come down and play with you," said the hermit. "His home is in the sky."

"Then who'll keep my secrets and hold me in the night and love me as I am? Who'll teach me and explain things and be my best friend? Where will *my* home be?"

"Some of us make our homes where we find them," said the hermit, tapping his borrowed shell. "What matters is that you are safe and cared for and loved."

Then Bear understood.

He ran home as fast as he could and climbed into Clara's big, soft bed.

And as they fell asleep, he told
her about everyone he had met and
all that had happened to him and

how he had been looking for someone
he already had.

About the Author/Illustrator

CLAY CARMICHAEL grew up in Chapel Hill, North Carolina. When she was small, she painted pictures in a tiny room called the art room over her grandmother's kitchen.

In school, she wrote stories and poems. She studied at Hampshire College and at The University of North Carolina, where she was awarded highest honors for her poetry.

She began *Bear at the Beach* one summer after her father became very sick. She wrote and painted some of it on an island in a house by the sea with the help of Bear, her lifelong friend.

She lives with two spoiled cats in Carrboro, North Carolina.